W9-BZU-607

LIMPOPO
THE
LION

A TALE OF LAZINESS AND LETHARGY

Published in 2010 by Windmill Books, LLC
303 Park Avenue South, Suite # 1280, New York, NY 10010-3657

Adaptations to North American Edition © 2010 Windmill Books
Copyright © Diverta Ltd 2009

CREDITS:
Text by Felicia Law
Illustrated by Lilli Messina

Library of Congress Cataloging-in-Publication Data

Law, Felicia.
  Limpopo the lion : a tale of laziness and lethargy / Felicia Law ; illustrated by Lilli Messina.
    p. cm. – (Animal fair values)
  Includes a note to teachers and parents and facts about lions.
  ISBN 978-1-60754-804-1 (library binding) – ISBN 978-1-60754-808-9 (pbk.) – ISBN 978-1-60754-812-6 (6-pack)
  [1. Lions–Fiction. 2. Self-reliance–Fiction.] I. Messina, Lilli, ill. II. Title.
  PZ7.L41835Li 2010
  [E]–dc22
                            2009038753

Manufactured in the United States of America

CPSIA Compliance Information: Batch #BW01W: For further information contact Windmill Books, New York, New York at 1-866-478-0556.

LIMPOPO
THE
LION

A TALE OF LAZINESS AND LETHARGY

FELICIA LAW
ILLUSTRATED BY LILLI MESSINA

alphabet
s o u p

an imprint of
WINDMILL BOOKS
New York

Limpopo was a lion

4

a great tawny, shaggy lion
the color of dry
African grass.

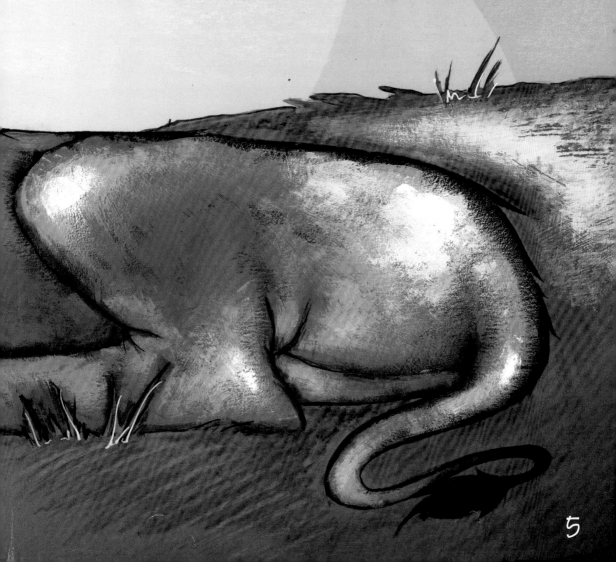

When he rested – **which he did a lot** – he was like a king on a throne, a magnificent carved lion, guarding a temple.

And when he stood – **which he did less often** – his huge back rippled with muscle and his roar was the call of the mighty ruler, demanding obedience from everyone on the vast plains.

Yes, Limpopo was a very handsome lion.
He was also **lazy** and **proud**.
He had decided long since that he wouldn't
lift a paw to do anything.
His **three wives** looked after
him and Limpopo liked this arrangement.

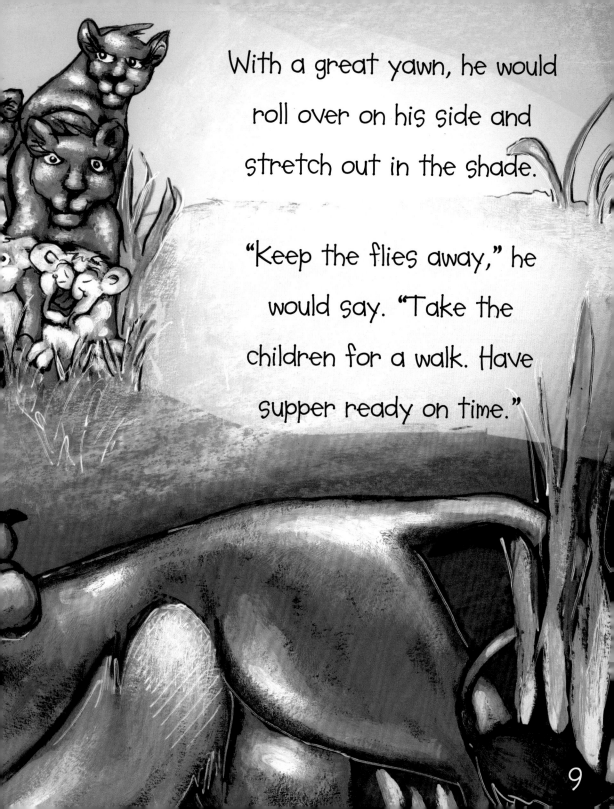

With a great yawn, he would roll over on his side and stretch out in the shade.

"Keep the flies away," he would say. "Take the children for a walk. Have supper ready on time."

9

His wives always chose the shadiest spot for him to rest.

They kept everyone quiet while he slept.
They brought up the children and trained
them to respect their father.

They hunted for his supper...

...and always had it ready when he woke.

And, in return Limpopo would let out the occasional ROAR...

to protect his family from danger.

Then one day everything changed!

It was the day the wives heard the gossip

from the **wildebeests**.

They were creeping up on the herd,
moving downwind and low on their stomachs
so the wildebeests wouldn't know they
were coming.

"Those poor lionesses! You have to pity them," the one wildebeest said. "They are slaves to that man."

"All day and every day, caring for the home,
bringing up the children, keeping food on the
table, making sure he's comfortable.
Have you ever seen him lift a paw to help?
Ha – not him!"

The wives looked at each other...

Had they ever seen him lift a paw to help?
No, they hadn't – not once – but it
sounded like a very good idea to them.

"He could help with the cleaning up,"
one wife suggested.
"Take the children to school," said another.
"Pack his own lunch," added a third.
"He wouldn't know where to begin,"
they agreed.

"He's absolutely useless without us."

19

That was the day the wives decided
to pack their bags and take the children
on a long vacation

without Limpopo...

Limpopo quickly discovered he didn't know
what to do on his own.

He asked the hyenas to bring him food,
but when the food arrived, it was clear
the hyenas had eaten all the best parts.

He asked the oxpeckers to groom his shaggy mane, but they pulled out hairs for their nests — and it hurt.

No one seemed to have much time to help Limpopo, and he soon lost his glossy, plump look and became rather sad and bedraggled.

And although he wouldn't admit it,
he was a teeny bit lonely too.

In fact, by the time the wives came back from vacation, things were looking pretty bad for Limpopo.

26

His wives were plump. Limpopo had not been there to eat most of the food, (and the best parts). His wives were smart. They had spent their time grooming themselves, (and not their lazy husband).

It was clear that things had to change. Limpopo moaned a little, but when he finally started to help with the chores, the best bits of meat started to come his way again.

29

And before long, Limpopo the lion had learned that if you pull your weight to help others, others will pull their weight to help you.

LEARN MORE

ABOUT THE LION

Limpopo is a pretend lion. Here are some facts about real lions.

- Lions are powerful predators. They are at the top of the food chain.
- Lions live in family groups called prides.
- A lion may live with several lionesses. There is usually just one adult male since the younger males leave the pride when they are fully grown.
- Lions have the strongest social bonds of all cats.
- The female lions hunt together. The male rules the home, but does not usually join the hunting.
- The male lion's main roles are to protect territory, females and young, and scare off hostile animals.

ABOUT LAZINESS AND LETHARGY

Limpopo the Lion deals with the consequences of laziness. If you are lazy and don't pull your weight, you can end up depending upon other people. This can make you weaker rather than stronger. You may feel like you're in charge because other people are doing things for you, but you can lose your independence.

Laziness can affect how we treat other people. We can become bossy and less aware of other people's needs.

Being a hard worker, self-reliant, and considerate of other people produces better results for individuals, and for a group!

Glossary

Gossip (GAH-sip) talking about rumors

Lethargy (LEHTH-ehr-gee) state of being lazy, inactive, and having no energy

Oxpecker (AWKS-pek-er) a small African bird that eats ticks off of larger animals

Tawny (TAH-nee) shade of brown tinged with yellow

Wildebeest (WILL-da-beest) stocky African mammal, also called a gnu

Index

FOR MORE INFORMATION

Books

Glassman, Bruce. *Responsibility*. New York: Rosen Publishing, 2009.

Kalman, Bobbie. *The life cycle of a lion*. New York: Crabtree Publishing Company, 2006.

Spilsbury, Richard. *Life in a pride of lions*. Chicago: Heinemann Library, 2005

Web Sites

To ensure the currency and safety of recommended Internet links, Windmill maintains and updates an online list of sites related to the subject of this book. To access this list of Web sites, please go to www.windmillbooks.com/weblinks and select this book's title.

For more great fiction and nonfiction, go to www.windmillbooks.com.